The Oracle of Philadelphia

THE
ORACLE
OF
PHILADELPHIA

A. S. PETERSON

TALES OF AN UNREMEMBERED COUNTRY

Cover design © 2014 by Chris Stewart
Illustrations © 2021 by Stephen Hesselman

Published by
Rabbit Room Press
3321 Stephens Hill Lane
Cane Ridge, TN 37013
info@rabbitroom.com

ISBN: 9781951872113

More things are wrought by prayer
than this world dreams of.

ALFRED LORD TENNYSON

Trumpets blared. Wives wept. Children laughed and ran. Investors shouted weak hurrahs and sweated through their stiff tailcoats, and on a nearby rooftop, a banker in a black hat overturned a bucket of confetti; its white flakes fluttered in the summer wind and drifted down on the well-wishers gathered at the Halifax waterfront.

The *Maribel Lynne* eased away from the wharf and turned swiftly toward the long silence ahead of her. She struck southeast for the Atlantic, but inside of two days she would come around to the north, and then, rushing past Newfoundland, would strike into the Labrador Sea. From there she would set her aim on the perilous latitudes of the Arctic in order to search out the Passage and all the wealth and acclaim that awaited whomever should discover it.

The discovery of that northwestern way was the purpose for which she had been built. Her oaken hull was nearly a foot thick at the waterline, engineered to withstand the crushing grip of ice. She wore skirts and bands of iron to rebuff and cleave a frozen sea. She was bloated with stores enough to sustain a small army for a year, and she was crewed by eighty-three men long of beard, strong of heart, and assured of her success.

But though the *Maribel Lynne's* virtues were many, it was in the confident seamanship of Captain Nathan Winthrop that the crew—not to mention the bucket-dumping banker, and the sweaty investors—had placed their faith. An Englishman by blood, Nathan Winthrop had been born abroad aboard a whaler among the icebergs of the Antarctic (his mother had been a harpooner of some

renown—she was speared by a narwhal at the age of 87 and died at sea of the ensuing sepsis). Russian pirates marooned the toddling Winthrop in the Aleutians at the age of three, and thereafter he was raised by a roving colony of pinnipeds. In his twenties he circumnavigated the globe twice over and named twelve islands after himself and the children he intended to one day father. In May of 1771 the *New-England Courant* reported that he once wrestled a polar bear bare-handed until it surrendered its coat and limped away hypothermic. Those who knew him said he kept a razor-sharp walrus-tooth knife in his boot, and he told anyone who asked that it was a gift from a great walrus chieftain who had once saved his life. If anything certain can be said of the *Maribel Lynne's* captain, it can be said that he was a man of extremes, and if any captain was to sail through the ice of the Arctic and discover the Northwest Passage, Nathan Winthrop was the one to do it—though some argued that because he was a man of southern seas, his Aleutian childhood notwithstanding, the ice of the opposite pole would surely stop him cold.

When the *Maribel Lynne* rode out of the Halifax harbor and into the Northern Atlantic, Captain Winthrop stood atop the forecastle of the ship with one boot propped on the forward rail. One of his fists gripped his shark-leather belt, his other was raised to the whalebone pipe between his pink lips, and his polar-bear coat flowed behind him like the robe of an ancient king. He struck awe into those who saw him, and he expected the sea to part at his coming. His golden beard shone.

To join their unfailing captain, the crew had come from all over the Upper and Lower Canadas as well as the American colonies. Bold seamen flowed toward Halifax like tributaries to a great river. They left their homes behind and climbed onto the ship's new-hewn decks for all manner of reasons: Tobias Sandemeyer joined for fortune and glory. Isaac Nettles out of simple boredom. Tomas Clemons hoped to bank a wealth of experience that only a such an expedition could earn. Jessup Styce had sailed under Captain Winthrop for eight years and hoped for his long-delayed promotion to bosun's mate. Richard and Samuel Timmons signed on to escape what they described as "a tiresome life wed to a plowshare."

But of all the eighty-odd men who crewed the *Maribel Lynne*, Thurston was the only soul to come aboard for love of a woman, though it must be said that he had greatly miscalculated Belinda Lee's challenge that she'd "only have a man who's made a name for himself." Had Thurston asked Belinda Lee to clarify her statement, she'd have happily added: "by which I mean, he should get a steady and respectable job"— by which she meant almost anything other than sailoring. Thurston, however, did not ask for such clarification. Instead, he signed aboard Captain Nathan Winthrop's expedition, hoping to have his name, along with those of his captain and his crewmates, writ forever in the annals of history. Thurston was a man of grand miscalculations—and aboard the *Maribel Lynne* he would soon to meet his match.

A BRISK WIND CARRIED THE SHIP FOR FOUR SUNNY days. But soon after her northwestern turn, week upon week of gloomy weather harrowed her and held her captive to whims of fickle winds that left her bobbing for days at a time, slack-sailed and helpless, accompanied only by the slosh of a viscous sea.

Five weeks after the fanfare of her embarkation, the winds again turned lively. The sails lifted and the fog scattered away, but the clear air reached only so far. It ended in a pale belly of cloud that loomed overhead. And on the following morning, the men of the *Maribel Lynne* spotted forerunners of the Arctic icepack.

A white horde of shabby floes drifted out of the north, enveloping the ship a piece at a time. Thurston looked down at the grey sea and considered it with a thoughtful frown. He had not expected ice so soon. According to his investigations into the matter, they should not have encountered the pack for two months or more, and not until farther north—but there it plainly floated. Pancake ice speckled the surface of the water. Hundreds of floes surrounded them, some no larger than life boats, others expansive enough to seem like small islands, and others still piled up in dirty white tiers having been rafted upon one another by forces of nature. Each slab of ice was raggedly round and curled up at its edges where it had been repeatedly battered and shaped by collisions with neighboring floes.

As Thurston watched, one of the smaller floes drifted near the ship and collided with the hull. The *Maribel Lynne* shuddered mildly. The ice cracked into pieces that tumbled aft along the hull and spun lazily in the ship's wake. Thurston looked on this small drama with great interest. He noted the ship's resilience and the relatively weak show of the ice in the encounter, and thus comforted, he went below decks and slept easily in the assurance of the *Maribel Lynne's* eventual victory.

Neither did Captain Winthrop pay any heed to the encroachment of the ice, even though it had come upon them far south of its expected latitude. He ordered his desk set on the quarterdeck and there he sat with an ancient wood-bound codex and studied its charts and secrets. He pored over the tome with terrifying intensity and looked up at intervals to scowl with a clenched brow at the northern horizon. When the first mate, a Spaniard called "Don" Fuego, asked the captain whether they should turn aside because of the ice, Winthrop answered in a dark growl, "Our way lies west or north or nowhere at all."

They pressed onward into the unseasonably cold summer. But the pack thickened about them slowly and silently, and in two weeks' time it closed its fist on the ship and held her fast. Enraged, Captain Winthrop leapt onto the ice. He flung back his white coat, ground his mighty teeth, and stabbed at the ice maniacally with his ivory knife. He carved out a fist-sized piece and ate it, crunching it and grinding

it into submission with his teeth. When the crew saw that their captain was yet the master of the ice, they were emboldened. They hurried over the rails and set out with picks and axes and augurs to split a lead in the pack through which the *Maribel Lynne* could advance.

The ship was caught in a field no more than half a mile across. Men ranged out in a column reaching all the way to the hard line of black water lapping at the edge of the floe. They sang and swung their axes and picks in time. The ice beneath their feet hummed and vibrated with the rhythm of the song and axe. Little by little they cut through the floe in chips and chunks.

To Thurston's thinking, the task was ill conceived. Not two hundred yards south of the ship, clear sea awaited them, but to the north and west, the ice stretched out for hundreds more yards, promising an entire day of hard labor, if not two. But with his reservations intact, he took his place in line and heaved his pick at the ice. In his preoccupation with second-guessing the captain's plans, he failed to swing his pick in correct time with the other men and came only a hair from decapitating the man opposite him. Thurston pulled his pick back hastily and spewed out a flustered apology.

"Hooooo! Hooooo!" said the nearly beheaded man. He jerked his own pick out of the ice and stood up laughing. "Heeheeheee! Heehee!" His high-pitched, staccato laugh sounded to Thurston like the mating call of an exotic bird.

"Thank the Lord for my poor aim," said Thurston. "It won't happen again. I swear it." The men to Thurston's left and right eyed him warily and shuffled wide.

"Naw, you ain't even come close." The man's voice, like his laugh, was an octave too high, and it leapt out of him with the quality of music, full of dips and heights, his syllables tumbling over one another like a run of notes. "I doubt you could nick me if you aimed to." The man rubbed the back of his neck with one hand and stuck the other out toward Thurston. "John Obadiah—like the New and Old Testy-ment all heaped up into one."

The man's cheekbones, which were mostly covered in hair, pinched upward, and his eyes narrowed.

Thurston inferred that behind the man's voluminous beard, he was smiling. He accepted Obadiah's hand and shook it. "Thurston," he said.

Obadiah laughed riotously and pumped Thurston's hand. "I'm thirsty too!" He produced a flask, drew on it, and then offered it to Thurston, who shook his head in refusal. "I reckon you ain't so thirsty after all. You go heave on with that pick. I'll swing after you so you ain't got to worry 'bout nickin' off John's noggin."

Thurston hefted his pick onto his shoulder and looked at the ship and then away at the ice field. "This is damned foolishness," he muttered. "We ought to be hauling her back out that way. It's no sense in going forward." Thurston slung his pick into the ice half-heartedly. "Can't he see that?"

John Obadiah swung his pick down. It made a satisfying thunk in the ice and he chuckled. "Any fool can go back-erds," said John in his wheezy high-pitched voice. "But Captain Winthrop it'n no fool. He sees the way forwards better'n you. Better'n me too. Look-it him up yonder."

Captain Winthrop had climbed into the crow's

nest of the mainmast and was looking northwest through a brass spyglass. The man's bold physique and the particular set of his pose as he studied the lie of the ship made him look as if he'd come to life from the back of an ancient coin, or was, perhaps, a marble statue of some Greek myth given gifts of flesh and blood.

"He's a damned fool," said Thurston. He swung his pick down and a deep cracking sound ran through the ice. Thurston stepped backward and watched as the ice floe shuddered and a thin line appeared at his feet. The line lengthened and widened and then all at once, with a noise like a thunderclap, the ice split clean apart and the Arctic Sea swirled and gurgled in the gap. The *Maribel Lynne* bobbed freely in the water and a cheer rang out from the crew. In the crow's nest, Captain Winthrop snapped his spyglass shut and howled like a wolf singing to the moon.

John Obadiah patted Thurston on the back as they walked toward the freed ship. "All aboard, Thursty."

Thurston didn't answer. He clambered aboard the *Maribel Lynne* in silence.

The weather warmed, the ice retreated, and the *Maribel Lynne* sailed onward, wending a mazelike path among the floes, ever slowly, but ever northward, and ever westward. Thurston felt more certain each week that they would indeed discover the Passage. He spent his days calculating how long it might be before he found himself in Halifax once more and could present himself (and the name he'd made) to Belinda Lee, and how she'd smile at him and agree at last to be wedded. But in late September, the ice reached out and seized them again. The temperature sank and no matter how much ice the captain ate, the crew could see no way through the pack to clear sea. After consulting the sky and the barometer and a pile of thirteen trustworthy almanacs—as well as his ancient codex—the captain felt assured that the weather would warm, the ice would thin, and the *Maribel Lynne* would be free again to pursue her goal. So the crew settled in. They kept below decks and played at cards and dice and huddled around stoves to keep warm.

As the weeks rolled on, Thurston began to crack his journal and make brief accounts for each of the days.

October 12th: Cold. We're ice-locked yet. Cards in the morning. Cards in the afternoon. 3rd watch with Obadiah.

October 13th: Cold. Ice-locked. More cards. Plenty of sleep. 3rd watch with Obadiah.

October 14th: Colder. Still ice-locked. Dice for a change. Sleep. 3rd watch with Obad . . .

"Whatchoo scribblin' in that book, Thursty?"

"It's a journal."

"Whatchoo scribblin' in that journal, Thursty?"

Thurston pointed his pencil out at the ice and swept his arm around to encompass the entire world about them. "This."

"Heck. You ain't need no journal to 'member all *this*, do you?"

Thurston silently resumed his journal entry:

> *October 14th:* Colder. Still ice-locked. Dice for a change. Sleep. 3rd watch with Obad . . . John Obadiah sees no sense in recordkeeping.

THE FOLLOWING DAY, THURSTON ARRIVED ON DECK for 3rd watch and John Obadiah said, "You scribblin' again?" Obadiah pointed his pipe out at the ice and swept his arm around to encompass the entire world about them. "Ain't you 'member all this since yestiddy?"

> *October 15th:* Beginning to agree with Obadiah.

Thurston gave up his documentation of the voyage, but only for a short time, for in the numbness of cold and monotony, he discovered that there was one subject that reliably captured his attention and provoked an almost endless sense of fascination, and, at times, something like scientific delight.

October 21st: Obadiah cleaned his ears for four hours. The result? A finely waxed mustache.

October 23rd: Obadiah smells like a pig two weeks dead. When questioned: "A pig two-week dead cain't smale at all!"

October 24th: Obadiah told me today that his grandfather was in the Bible. The book of 3rd Romans, he reckons. He also reckons that if he's lucky, one day they might write him into it as well. Second Obadiah, one assumes (or 4th John?).

October 28th: Asked Obadiah if he could read. He said he'd never tried but thought he probably could since his "Grandy Pap" was a preacher. I offered to put him to the test but he said that "even Jesus tole the Devil it wudn't right to be tested," so he declined on "thay-o-LAW-jee-cull principle." Conclusion: Obadiah cannot read.

October 30th: Freezing today. Obadiah thawed his beard after 3rd watch and claimed that the resulting "beard-squeezin's" are likely to have medicinal, and possibly magical,

J. Obadiah's

MEDICINUL

MAJICAL!

"GOOD FE
WAT AIL
YER"

RIPE!

PURE!

ARROW-
MATIC!

NATRUL

POTENT!

BAIRD SQUEEZINS

properties. He has captured nearly a pint of it in a bottle and intends to sell it once it has "ripened." Offered a taste: declined.

As Thurston's observations of John Obadiah continued, he found that while he enjoyed a strange fascination with the man, he also harbored a nascent revulsion. But Thurston was a learned man and concealed his distaste by thinking of himself in the vein of other great explorers of the natural world whose vocations had driven them to observe and document their subjects without judgment. John Obadiah was his subject, and Thurston busied himself with his every detail, noting schedules, curiosities of language and diet, and even drawing crude pictures of him in his "natural" habitat.

When winter fell, the world of the *Maribel Lynne* froze into a domain of wholly intractable ice; it grew in both thickness and expanse and would suffer no halt to its advance. Captain Winthrop alone withstood it. He sat daily at his desk on the quarterdeck and studied his charts and his tome. Don Fuego begged him to come below and keep warm, but Winthrop was born to the cold and it exercised no power over him. At the change of each watch, he assured the crew that their fortunes would improve. But each day, as Thurston looked around him, his faith in the captain's success grew fainter. The ship was caught in the teeth of the frozen sea, its jaws closing ever tighter around her belly. Every hour it became more apparent to Thurston (though not to Captain Nathan Winthrop) that only in the thaw of spring could the *Maribel Lynne* hope for her deliverance.

For months, the world without was no more than snow and wind and ice, and the world within little more than sleep, boredom, and a never-ending quest for warmth. Thurston busied himself with his studious observance of John Obadiah, a man whom he perceived to be in a eternal state of contentment. If Obadiah was cold, Thurston observed that he was satisfied to be so. If he was told to work, Thurston noted that he was eager do it, no matter the task. If he was hungry and the galley ran short on hot eats, Obadiah seemed happy to gnaw at a strip of dried beef instead. Never once did Thurston note a jot of unhappiness or anger in the man, nor did he ever seem ill at ease, or even low of spirit. While others pined for home, cursed the ice, and paced the lower decks of the ship in their restlessness, John Obadiah simply abided in a state of perpetual contentment—a state that Thurston came to abhor. He could account for his distaste of John's ease only by noting that he felt it was unnatural for any man to be so imperturbable in the face of such a cold and unyielding world as the polar winter offered.

They'd abandoned the warmer days of lesser latitudes when the *Maribel Lynne* sailed from Halifax in May. In the same way, they'd abandoned comfort and loved ones and even good food and dry land. But as winter tilted into its full stride, it was the sun that turned traitor, abandoning them to the frozen waste of the Arctic as if even light itself feared the bite of ice. The darkness of the ship's close spaces made ghosts even of hearty men, some retreating, pale and thin, into the corners to sleep for days or weeks at a time. Many called them "sleepers" and gave them wide berth for they mistrusted the animal nature of their long hibernations. At intervals, Don Fuego would report in solemn tones that a sleeper had gone "too deep" and had passed beyond slumber into death.

December stretched into January, January into February, February into a fever dream of prayers for light, until the sun rallied his courage, repented of his treachery, and began to chase the winter back into outer darkness. When March arrived, it felt no warmer, but with the return of light, the men began again to hope and the sleepers put off their drowse and rejoined the waking world of men. Thurston observed with irritation that John Obadiah weathered all this as if the creeping bleakness of winter had been no lesser a pleasure than the lusty delight of May.

In mid-April, Captain Winthrop gleaned from his tome and almanacs that the polar spring would soon be upon them. He sent out scouting parties to discover the extent of their prison and search for signs of their imminent release. Two men he sent in each of the four cardinal directions, and two more in each of the ordinals. When he came to the northwest he shouted "Thurston! Obadiah!"

The two men looked at one another, and John Obadiah grinned.

"Here I am!" shouted John.

Thurston frowned.

"Northwest with the two of you," said Captain Winthrop.

"Yes, sir," said John.

"Spy out the Passage, Obadiah. And get you back here." John Obadiah chuckled while he and the captain stared at one another briefly. The moment passed so quickly that Thurston doubted he'd seen it at all, but it seemed a silent conversation had passed between the two men and both had understood all that was said and agreed upon some unspoken point.

"Heave to," said the captain. "Get you all back inside the week and tell me how poorly we lay."

John slapped Thurston on the back. "Look like it's you and me, Thursty."

"So it does." Thurston walked to the rail and looked northwest. It was ice as far as he could see. He went below to pack supplies and, an hour later, met John on the ice where a sled had been allotted to them. Thurston lashed his pack and equipment to the sled and turned to John Obadiah.

"Where's your pack?" Thurston asked.

"I kin get along without one. Ain't but extry to carry."

"What about food?"

"It'n you brought some?"

"Rations for myself. Not for two."

"I allow we'll make do."

"What about clothes?"

"Wearing 'em!"

"You're a damned fool."

"So I been tole. Lemme hitch up that sled, Thursty. I'll shoulder it." John lifted the sled's harness, settled it over his shoulders, and fastened the buckle across his chest. "We ready!"

Thurston stared long and hard at his partner. The man was dressed in a cobbled together outfit of rabbit, otter, and fox fur, and he'd covered his head with a cap of tattered coonskin. His beard grew high on his cheekbones such that little more than eyes and a red patch of nose showed forth in a great expanse of hair (both human and animal). The eyes twinkled, and they held not an ounce of trepidation for the journey ahead. John Obadiah was eager, and the fact of it unsettled Thurston. It had been one thing to observe and document the strange creature and his peculiars, but to go forth at his side into the peril of the polar north and admit the prospect that both of their lives may rely each upon the other—that was another matter.

Thurston looked from his sled, to the ice-fast ship, to his partner, to the ice field before them. "We are going to die," he said.

"Die? Naw. Come on, Thursty. Let's go find the captain his Passage." John hollered out something that sounded like the whooping of a tropical bird and trotted off with the sled in tow.

Thurston looked back at the *Maribel Lynne*. Captain Winthrop was hunched over the rail, scanning the horizon for a way free of the ice. His great polar bear coat hung around his shoulders and flowed to the deck, making it seem a snow bank had formed around him. Thurston turned away from the ship and followed John Obadiah into the ice field.

THE SHIP DWINDLED INTO THE DISTANCE, AND Thurston and John Obadiah became explorers in a world of white. At first, the field around them seemed barren, bereft of feature, no more than a frozen blanket of sea without texture to hook the eye. But as they lumbered across the icescape, they began to perceive the subtleties of the polar cap. Thurston first noticed that the ice was not always white. Where it jutted up in sharp spikes it became translucent and green at its heart, or, sometimes, sapphire blue, and once they came upon a great slab washed so clean and clear that the sunlight splintered into tiny rainbows as it passed through the thickness of it. Pressure ridges had formed where floes collided and were subsumed or thrown skyward. The ridges often created towers that rose up from the field and loomed ominously like great sentinels of the polar frontier watching over their every step. Many of these seemed to Thurston to glow from within as if a living heart pulsed inside them. In other places, they came upon piles of shattered ice that lay scattered as if some antediluvian monstrosity had burst up from below to gulp in air before diving once more into the frigid darkness beneath their feet. A land of wonders unfolded around them, and soon Thurston dared not blink for fear of missing the appearance of some newly revealed majesty of the Arctic.

But though wonders lay all before and around him, Thurston continually looked back. The *Maribel Lynne* became a speck in the distance. It looked to Thurston like a dead housefly lying on a white windowsill. The ship's masts jutted up and scraped at the sky like upturned legs.

"Stop," said Thurston. When Obadiah failed to hear him, he said it again, shouting, "Stop!"

John eased the sled to a halt and turned. "You lonesome for home already?"

"We'll lose sight of the ship."

John looked from Thurston to the distant ship and then back to Thurston. "It'n that the point? If we don't lose sight of the ship, we can't see nothing the captain can't see from out his shiny peeper glass."

Thurston didn't answer. He bent over the sled and pulled out a wooden stake and a wad of red linen.

"Whatchoo doin', Thursty?"

"We have to know where we're going—and

where we've been. We can't use a compass, and the sun's a poor guide. If we don't mark our way before we lose sight of the ship, we won't be able to find our way back." Thurston tore off a strip of red cloth and held it in his mouth. He climbed atop a pressure ridge and began to hammer the stake into the ice at its peak. John Obadiah stared up at him, and the way his hairy cheeks twitched, Thurston could tell the man was grinning behind his beard.

"They ain't no worry to find our way back, Thursty. We just run in a straight line away from the *Maribel*, and when we get hungry to come back, we jest turn 'round and walk straight till we find her. We ain't need no biddy little flag."

Thurston ignored John and the grin fluttering behind his beard. He set the stake and tied the red strip of cloth around it. When he was satisfied, he climbed down and stuffed the wad of linen back into his pack.

John stared up at the stake in apparent mystification. "That's a mighty fine flag a flappin' up yonder, Thursty. I allow we shore won't get lost now. Hoohooohooo! Heheheee!" To Thurston, John's idiotic laugh sounded like nothing so much as the call of a common loon.

Thurston stood up and tried his best not to shout. "There's a woman back in Halifax, and I aim to marry her. I can't get back to her without I get back to Halifax. And I can't get back to Halifax without I get back to the *Maribel Lynne*." As Thurston laid into

his rant, John Obadiah's eye's got progressively wider. "And I fear I won't get back to the *Maribel Lynne* if I listen to another word out of your fool mouth, John Obadiah! When we get back alive, I suggest you thank Captain Winthrop for sending me along with you. I have no doubt you'd be lost and dead and never seen again if it weren't for my 'mighty fine flag a flappin'!'" By the time Thurston was done, John's eyebrows had crawled up so far they'd disappeared amongst the coon fur on his head.

"All right, all right, Thursty. I thank yeh for raising that biddy little flag up yonder. You give a holler when we need another little flag raised up and I'll even hep you pound her in."

"Shut up and pull the sled."

Obadiah's beard twitched and quivered. Thurston suspected he was being grinned at again, but before he could be sure, John turned and leaned into the sled's harness and off he went, trotting briskly.

An hour later, the wind picked up. When it began to snow as well, Thurston judged another flag was prudent, and John kept true to his word to help him set it. When they were done, Thurston stood by the flag and stared into the distance behind them. He craned his neck from side to side and held his hand up to shield the ice glare from his eyes and blinked and stared until his eyes watered and then he said: "I can't see the other flag." He stole a glance at John and saw the unmistakable signs of a hidden smirk. Thurston turned to the right and scanned the ice field, narrowing his eyes and working methodically across his field of vision from left to right, near to far, searching for the one ridge of ice topped with a tiny red flag. When he failed to find it, he turned to his left to begin again, thinking he'd gotten turned around somehow. As he swept his head toward John he caught the almost imperceptible movement of his shoulders. They were gently shaking up and down. "You think this is funny?" yelled Thurston.

"Naw, Thursty. I allow it it'n no funny a'tall. Heeehehehehee!"

Thurston stomped over to the sled and untied his pack. He threw it down on the ice and tore it open. "We'll camp here. It'll clear up in the morning and we'll see it."

John sat down on the ice and pulled a strip of dried beef out of his pocket. He sniffed at it suspiciously then tore a piece off and chewed it while he watched Thurston lay out the tent. "You want some hep with that tent, Thursty?"

Thurston didn't answer. The wind picked up and began to howl and by the time he had the first tent stake in the ice, the whole canvas was flapping in the wind like an unsheeted sail. Thurston laid himself bodily on the tent to hold it down while he hammered in the second stake. John Obadiah watched patiently.

"Shore you wouldn't like some hep with that tent, Thursty?"

Thurston ignored the offer, but he could hear the constant *smack-smack* of John chewing away at his beef, and the sound very nearly drove him to unpleasantness. When Thurston got the third tent stake in, the canvas agreed to be managed and in a further few minutes the tent was up and snow was piling against its windward side. Thurston dragged his pack into the tent, spread his pallet out on the ice, laid back, and closed his eyes while weariness crept over him. He lay quietly for some time, letting his thoughts drift toward Belinda Lee and the promise of her warm embrace, but just as she was near enough to touch, his eyes shot open and he sat up.

"John!" Thurston shouted. "John, get in here." When he heard no answer, he crawled out of his tent and looked around. The wind had calmed, and a thick blanket of snow, far more than a few minutes worth, covered the tent and sled. Thurston realized he'd done more than merely drift toward sleep; he had slept for hours.

Thurston circled the tent, searching the ground. "John Obadiah!" he called out, but there was no answer. Dread took hold of him. "John!" he cried out again. He climbed up the pressure ridge to where he had staked the second flag. On the ridge beside the flag he discovered the form of a man sitting upright and cross-legged, shrouded entirely in snow. Thurston stumbled forward and shook John's shoulder. The snow fell away and John turned his head.

"Mornin', Thursty!" John shook his head like a

wet dog and the snow flew away from it. He stretched his mouth open and yawned loudly as the ice in his beard cracked and fell away in chunks.

"What are you doing out here?" said Thurston. "You'll freeze!"

"Naw. Cold don't bother me. Looky yonder." John pointed into the distance. Thurston looked and saw the previous flag flapping in the air like a wind-whipped flame. "You happy now, Thursty?"

"Let's go."

They packed the sled and traversed the ice in silence, stopping three times to set up new flags. Each time they did so, John Obadiah, assisted without dissent, but Thurston could tell by the bristling of the man's beard that his help was no more than an amusement.

That night, John offered to sleep outside once again and Thurston had to insist that he come into the tent. "You'll freeze. Get in here."

"I froze before. It weren't bad."

"I won't have your death on my conscience. Get in."

"Naw, you go on and cozy up."

Thurston flung the tent flap shut and threw himself down, but ten minutes later he was up again because his conscience wouldn't let him sleep with John outside.

"Get in here!"

"Dang, Thursty! Why you so aggervated!"

"Captain Winthrop told you to get back to the ship. He didn't say anything about freezing yourself to death on the ice. Now get in the damned tent!"

John stared at Thurston until the man sighed and crawled into the tent. The two men lay beside one another on their backs and stared silently up at the peak in the canvas overhead.

"I thank yeh, Thursty."

"Go to sleep." Thurston closed his eyes and John began to wriggle and writhe and scoot around like he had a snake in his pants. Thurston gritted his teeth. "*What* are you doing?"

"Got to get something out my pocket."

Thurston rolled onto his side and clenched his jaw until it hurt. John went still. There was a tearing sound, and then the *smack-smack* of John chewing on dried beef. All at once, Thurston was aware of everything he despised about John Obadiah—the musky scent of him, the wiry crumb-caked beard, the tiny pink nose, the lilting voice, the infuriating content-edness, the lack of concern for anything that didn't satisfy some base craving—like the beef between his teeth; Thurston could smell it, the sickly-sweet odor of beef reconstituting in the man's saliva. The *smack-smacking* filled the tent. In the darkness, Thurston's mind fixed itself on a vision of Obadiah's yellow teeth champing and stamping and grinding dead cow-flesh, the man's jaw working like a bellows, blowing the stench of old meat out into the close space of the tent. *Smack-smack-smack-smack-smack.* Just when Thurston thought he could stand it no longer, John Obadiah began to shake lightly. The movement was scarcely more than a tremble, but Thurston knew exactly what it meant. The man was laughing, quietly, to himself, as he champed his beef and fouled the air.

Smack-smack-smack-smack.

"What is *wrong* with you?"

Smack-sma—John froze.

The tent went silent. Thurston waited impatiently for an answer.

"Want me to tell you something, Thursty?"

"I want you to clap your mouth shut and go to sleep."

"You ever been to Philly-delphia?"

"What?"

"You ever been to Philly-*del*phia?"

Thurston kept silent. He took a deep breath and tried to calm himself.

"I been once," said John. "Captain Winthrop brung me with him to see the oracle."

"What the hell are you talking about?

"It's a funny story and I was jest thinking on it. You want to hear it?" John did not wait for Thurston's answer. "She don't see nobody but on Sunday afternoons in the summer-time, and when Captain Winthrop seen he

was bound for the Passage, he sent her a letter asking could he come to see her afore he left for Hally-fax. He brung me with him."

Thurston shook his head and resigned himself to hearing John out, hoping he'd quiet and go to sleep once he'd told his tale. "So the captain took you to Philadelphia? That's mighty fine, John."

"I ain't even got to the *good* part yet, Thursty."

"Well hurry it up."

Smack-smack-smack. "Captain Winthrop come and scooped me up to go with him so he could put the oracle to the test and see if she was enny good on account of she might be a common witch what can't be trusted. But she shore weren't. Me and the captain we got to Philly-delphia, and we went in this old church house what looked about as old as Methuselah and there she was. They was a whole bunch of folks. They filled up the pews, but they didn't seem like no church-goin' folk I ever seen before. They was singing and quaking like Quakers and mumbalin' words that wut'n no words I ever heard of. The captain said they was Spirit-took." *Smack-smack-smack.* "But them folks wasn't the main thing. That was the oracle. Captain tole me her real name was Cybil but nobody dared to call her that no more since she was the oracle and all. She was up at the pulpit like a preacher man—but she was a *woman!*" *Smack-smack-smack.* "And you know what else, Thursty?

"What else, John?"

"I'll tell you. She had snakes all over. She had a big red one wrapped up 'round her wrist, and she had another was crawled across her shoulders and was making its way down the front of her shirt—that worried me something awful. Ennyway, we watched her for a while and she was preachin' to the folks in the pews and they was quakin' and saying '*Amen!*' and she was carryin' on about how all the preachers do—except she done it with snakes." *Smack-smack-smack.* "And then she climbed on top a three-legged stool and an old lady come and put a pot under the stool and smoke come up out of the pot and covered all around the oracle and she asked if there was ennyone needed to come up and be *tole* something. That's when Captain Winthrop jumped up from his pew and drug me to see her. She looked down on us and I was turrible afraid of them snakes, Thursty.

41

Turrible afraid. She asked the captain why was we come, and the captain said he was come for a tellin' but for her to do the tellin' on me first so as he could see she wasn't a witch but was a real oracle same as

folks had a long time ago. So I went up by that crazy stool with her and all the folks in the church house was mumbalin' and carryin' on and she looked at me and smiled, only it wasn't a kind of smile you like to see too much, and then she bent over and asked me what I wanted her to tell." *Smack-smack-smack.*

Thurston rolled over onto his back. "What did you say?"

"I couldn't hardly see nothing but them snakes all over, and I was thinking to myself that I was liable to get snake-bit and die on the spot. So I said, "Tell me am I goin' to die?" And she smiled again and bent over and whispered in my ear and tole me something, and tole me that I wasn't to tell no one what it was she said.

"What did she tell you?"

"Ain't you jest *heard* me, Thursty? I *cain't* tell." *Smack-smack-smack.* "So ennyway, I went on down and the captain he asked me same as you. He said, 'What did you ask her to tell you?' and I tole him 'I asked her was I goin' to die?' and the captain said, 'Well, are you?' and I said, 'Yes . . . but not today I reckon. She tole me *how* I was goin' to die and I look around and it don't seem likely at the moment.' So the captain he thought about that, and then he pulled out his gun and shot me dead."

"He did *what*?"

"He shot me dead—only I *wasn't* dead. And that's how come he knew she wasn't a witch but was a real oracle."

"The captain shot you?"

"Durn shore did."

"Where did he shoot you?"

"In the head."

"In the head?"

"Right yonder on the noggin."

John raised his hand to his head but in the darkness Thurston could see no more than the general motion. "So what did she tell the captain?"

"He asked her the same thing: 'Was he goin' to die,' and she tole him somethin' in his ear and tole him the same as she did me that he wasn't to tell no one what it was. And then we left and come to Hally-fax."

"Huh."

"So don't you worry about getting lost, Thursty.

I ain't going to die out here. I been tole so by the oracle. And I won't let you die neither."

"That's comforting, John. Good night."

"Good night, Thursty."

THE FOLLOWING DAY, THEY TORE DOWN THE TENT, loaded the sled, and made headway into the north-west. At mid-day they planted the last of the stakes and continued on until Thurston dared not go any further for fear of losing sight of the final "flag a flappin'."

"That's it, John. We have to turn back," said Thurston.

John halted the sled and extricated himself from its harness. He looked back at the last marker and then turned and looked ahead of them. "But we ain't found nothin'."

"We're out of stakes. We can't go any farther."

John spat and turned northwest. He stood up on his tiptoes and looked at the horizon. "Think I see somethin'.

Thurston looked. He craned his neck and

squinted his eyes. "I don't see anything."

"That don't mean it ain't there. Come on, Thursty."

"We can't. If we go any further we may never get back."

"You stay there, then. I got to go see if somethin's there."

"What? No! We're turning back. *Now*." Thurston turned and walked toward the last flag.

"You ain't listened to *nothin'*, Thursty. Hold on, now."

Thurston stopped and hung his head.

"Sit yourself down. Let me run out yonder and have a look. You wouldn't leave me to die out here would yeh?" John's beard twitched. "Besides, the Cap'n shore will be sore if we ain't found nothin'."

"*Fine*. Go. But if you get out of eyeshot, don't expect me to come looking for you."

"Heheheee! I'll be back, Thursty. Don't you worry."

John Obadiah trotted away. Thurston sat down on the sled and watched him go. As John dwindled into the distance, it occurred to Thurston that the wind on his face was warmer than he'd felt since they set out from Halifax nearly nine months before. The warmth, which was really only a lesser cold, put Thurston in mind of Belinda Lee waving from the pier-side and looking none too happy about his departure. She'd said plenty of cold words about the extent of his plans to make a name for himself and wed her, but Thurston couldn't bring himself to violate his contract with Captain Winthrop and the expedition, and so all of her bitter words had come to be summed up in the forlorn look she gave him as the ship heaved away from the wharf. For Thurston, the thought of how that look was bound to change when the *Maribel Lynne* sailed back into the Halifax harbor was all he needed to keep himself warm, even in the deep polar winter that now lay behind him. He pulled off his gloves and rubbed his hands together, and then he noticed John out ahead of him jumping up and down and waving his arms wildly. Thurston waved back and John Obadiah began dancing a jig on the ice. He pumped his elbows in and out and kicked up snow and slapped at his knees and then jumped up and down again and swung his arm at Thurston as if to say, "Come on down, Thursty!"

Thurston squinted his eyes and looked around as if some other man might be the object of John's invitations. When Thurston didn't move to answer, John hooked his arm more and more enthusiastically. Thurston stood up and yelled, "*What?*" but the wind and distance soaked up his cry and kept it well out of John's earshot. Thurston shook his head and took a few steps forward. He looked back at the sled and pondered it until he was satisfied that it showed no signs of wanderlust. Then with a last shrug of his shoulders, he ran out to see what John had found.

When John Obadiah saw that Thurston had heeded his call, he recommenced his idiot's dance, and by the time Thurston had crossed the distance, both men were winded. Thurston drew up next to John and stood at the edge of the ice field. A deep black Arctic Sea stretched beyond him in gentle undulations.

"We done it, Thursty! We found Captain Winthrop his way out the ice! Hoooo! Heheheeehehe!" John pin-wheeled his arms and kicked up his heels and danced like a drunkard. Thurston bent over with his hands on his knees and tried to gather his breath. The sea ahead of him was clear of ice as far as he could see, and, as best as he could reckon it, directly to the northwest.

John slapped his leg and hooted. "Come on, Thursty! It's cause for dancin'!"

Thurston surprised himself by smiling. But before he could surprise himself by dancing, a great grey whale breached the surface not twenty feet from where he stood on the ice. The leviathan rose straight up out of the depths, yawned at the sky, then dove and threw its tail twenty feet up into the air. "Would you look at that," Thurston said. The whale's plunge sent a swell of seawater rolling toward them. Thurston and John backpedaled away from the edge of the ice as the wave swept over it and washed the ice clean under their feet. Both men laughed, and then they locked arms and danced around in a circle and sang as the whale breached the surface again a hundred yards distant. They paused their merriment to watch the whale's display, and when it was gone, another swell raced toward them. Water surged up over the ice and—

Crack.

"What was that?" asked Thurston.

Crack.

John's eyebrows crawled up toward his hairline and he looked around in awe. "You 'member what I tole you last night, Thursty?"

"About Philadelphia?"

"Jest you don't forget it."

"What? Why?"

CRACK.

The pack beneath their feet shuddered, and to their left a massive expanse of ice broke free and drifted away from them.

"The pack is breaking up." Thurston turned and looked back toward the sled just as a series of sharp *pops* split the air. A ragged crack shot through the ice.

"Get to the sled!" said John. They ran and the ice shuddered and split around them. Fissures opened and seawater seethed within the widening gaps. Behind them the ice field broke into dozens of smaller floes that bumped and shattered against one another. When they reached the sled, John buckled on the harness.

Thurston shouted, "Go, go!"

John Obadiah's smile was so big that Thurston could see it gleaming through the man's beard like a sun risen behind trees. "Go!" cried Thurston.

"Cool your britches, Thursty. They ain't no hurry."

The ice trembled under Thurston's feet.

"Are you insane?"

"You ain't listened to a *thang* I said, did you?"

The floe shuddered and buckled, and Thurston pushed the sled and yelled, "Go now or we'll be killed!"

"That oracle tole me how I was to die. And what she tole me ain't had nothing to do with ice and cold and all *this*." John Obadiah casually pointed out at the ice and swept his arm around to encompass the entire world about them. "So quit your squallin."

"Oracle? An *oracle* told you? You are a blame idiot, John Obadiah!"

Another crack opened with a series of sharp pops and shot across the ice field. Beside John, a massive slab of ice broke away, and, unbalanced by the shifting weight of the broken pack, it upended and rolled in the seething water. One end plummeted and the other shot fifteen feet into the air. Thurston watched slack-jawed as the slab paused at its apex, tottered, and then descended toward them. John Obadiah didn't move, but in an instant, Thurston's eyes jumped from the slab hurtling toward him, to the ground, to John; the geometry was plain as day—he would either move or be crushed. Thurston leapt out of the way as the ice descended. He rolled over just in time to see the unmistakable twitch of John's beard as the ice came down.

"John!"

The sled was gone, crushed beneath a heaping mound of shattered ice. Thurston ran to the other side of the ice heap and found John waiting with his arms crossed, his grin flamboyant in his beard. "Ain't I *tole* you?" he said.

Thurston looked from John to the ice and back again. He judged that the ice floe could not have missed him by more than a hair's breadth.

John turned away and walked in the direction of the ship. "Come on, Thursty."

Thurston tugged at the remnants of his pack protruding out from under the fallen ice, and then he gave up and followed Obadiah.

"Do you see the flag?"

"I seen it."

"Where?"

"Yonder."

Thurston squinted his eyes and looked across the ice. A tiny spot of red stood out in the distance. "I see it. Let's go." With a last glance behind him at the ice breaking and rafting to the northwest, Thurston sped his pace and ran for the marker.

By the time they reached the flag, Thurston's breath had got well away from him and it took him the better part of half an hour to be sure he had it back. He looked mournfully toward the crushed sled far behind them and considered that with no tent, there would be no shelter for the night.

"We have to keep on," said Thurston. "We've got to keep pace while we have the light. Then we walk right on through the night. If we stop, we'll freeze to death before morning."

John grinned and shrugged, and Thurston walked on ahead while John followed.

Before dark, they reached three more markers, and Thurston, scarcely able to move, collapsed to his knees. He shivered and clapped his hands together. "Can't stop. We'll freeze," he said through his chattering teeth.

John knelt down beside him and unbuttoned his otter fur coat. He opened the coat wide, revealing a raggedy, sweat-soaked yellow shirt beneath it. "Come on, Thursty. Climb on in here."

Thurston recoiled in disgust and crawled into the lee of the pressure ridge on which the flag was staked. "We'll just stop and rest for a bit. Just a bit."

"You go on get some sleep, Thursty."

Thurston didn't answer. He pulled his knees up and hugged his coat to his chest and let his eyes close. He saw Belinda Lee come toward him. She walked across the ice, deftly and surely, almost as if she were performing some strange slow dance. The wind and cold didn't seem to worry her or even toss her hair. When she was close enough that Thurston could smell the goodness of her, she sat down on a stool and frowned at him. A thick smoke rose up around her and she scolded him for the foolishness of joining the expedition. Then, inexplicably, she pulled a luxurious fur coat out of the bodice of her dress as easily as a magician pulls coins out of a young boy's ear. She bent over and wrapped the coat around Thurston, and he leaned in to embrace her. She was all warmth and scents of spring: jasmine, lilac, cherry blossom. Thurston inhaled deeply of the long-absent perfume of her, but the breath caught in his throat and he awoke in a fit of coughing to discover himself swaddled in otter hide and held firmly against John Obadiah's chest.

Thurston cried in alarm and hurled himself out of the coat and into the cold. The sun was up and John was giggling. "Don't you get aggervated, Thursty!"

Thurston stood up and staggered around, still haunted by the possibility that Belinda Lee might be somewhere nearby. "Where is she?"

John's eyebrows climbed up his forehead and he looked around suspiciously. "Where's who?"

Thurston shook his head and rubbed his eyes. He inspected himself, patting his chest and sides as if he'd lost a pocket watch or some other valuable. "Nevermind." He threw a vehement look at John and said, "Stay *away* from me. Where are we?"

Thurston scrambled up the ridge to the flag and searched the southeast for the fifth marker. Obadiah dug around in his pocket and pulled out a strip of beef. He tore it, stuffed a wad in his mouth, and began to smack on it. Then he climbed up the ridge, and offered the other half to Thurston.

Thurston pushed John's hand away in irritation. "There's the next mark," he said.

John stopped his smacking and looked. "Where at?"

Thurston pointed again and saw something that paled his face. The marker had moved. The relationship of its position to the ridges of ice around it had subtly shifted. The flag had moved northward.

"Flag's on the move," said John matter-of-factly.

"That's impossible."

"Naw. The ice is breakin' up, driftin', pulled north by the Indrawin' Sea." John chuckled and scratched his nose. "I tole you them bitty little flags was silly."

"Indrawing Sea?"

John shrugged. "I seen it in the captain's book— the old one he got—and he tole me all about it. He said at the Pole they's a big black mountain of iron and all around it is the Indrawin' Sea. Pulls everything down a big swirlin' hole to the middle of the world."

Thurston narrowed his eyes and stared at John. John chawed his beef and shrugged. If John had anything more to say, Thurston intended to ignore it entirely. He climbed down the ridge and walked toward the drifting flag, John hummed to himself, climbed to his feet, and followed.

An hour later, they came to the edge of the ice. The flag, flapping happily in the wind, was on a small floe a hundred yards distant. A cold black sea spanned the intervening distance.

John patted Thurston on the back and pointed to a floe adrift further distant yet. Atop it, Thurston could just make out another flicker of red.

"We're done for."

"Naw. Come on," said John.

"Where? How? You still don't understand do you? Our only point of reference is that flag, John. And now it's gone afloat. We can't get to it! We don't know where it was. Or how far it's moved! Do you understand? We're lost!"

John's beard shook and his cheeks pinched up as he giggled. "I *tole* you them biddy little flags was silly. Now come on, Thursty. We jest got to go by dead reckonin'. That's that only way I know to get around ennyhow."

John jogged away and Thurston stared after him, trying desperately to think of a course of action that didn't involve following John Obadiah and his dead reckoning, but with no other option apparent, he cursed the ice, spat on it, and ran after John. They followed the ice in a southerly direction when they could and turned in an easterly direction when possible. Thurston kept on John's heels. They stopped twice to smack on dried beef but otherwise took no rest. By mid-day they were too tired to do more than shamble and shuffle and raise their heads from time to time to see if the *Maribel Lynne* was in sight. The breaking of the icepack continued. They often leapt across leads of water between floes, and sometimes had to backtrack when the floe they traversed had drifted too far from the next. And though they saw no more of Thurston's flags, on they went, John leading, Thurston dismal behind.

At the end of the day they spotted the *Maribel Lynne*. The ice, however, had delivered her a mortal bite. In the months of her captivity, the frozen sea had gnawed at her until, in the end, it had worked a single tooth through her oaken hide. The breach was hidden in the bowels of the lower bilge and no one, not even Captain Winthrop, had known she was pierced until the pack broke up, the jaws loosened, and the sea rushed into her empty belly. As the ice released her from its grip, she groaned in the pangs of death.

The crew was ranged around her on the ice, watching her creak and shudder and die. John and Thurston were too late to do more than watch, and they could not approach, for the ice between them and the ship had already gone out. They would have to circle around to the south to reach the ship, and so they saw the entire affair from a small peninsula of ice protruding out from the main pack. As Thurston looked on, he saw Captain Winthrop standing proudly at the helm. His polar bear coat enshrouded him. His beard glistened in the sunlight. He peered through his spyglass even as the ship sank beneath him.

"He means to go down with her," said Thurston as he solemnly dragged his hat off his head and held it over his heart. Captain Winthrop turned toward them with his spyglass and stopped. He lowered the glass and looked in their direction, then he raised the glass again and looked their way once more before lifting his hand and waving. John Obadiah waved back.

"He seen me," said John.

The *Maribel Lynne* rolled over onto her side and pitched Captain Winthrop into the sea. The water around the ship churned and roiled as it pushed the air from her lungs. She rolled again and her keel rose up out of the water. She shuddered and bobbed and then descended into the depths, the keel slipping smoothly out of sight like the dorsal fin of great Leviathan. The surface of the sea rippled momentarily and then calmed. Nothing more was ever seen of the *Maribel Lynne*. In the sea around the site of her demise, her crew was stranded, piecemeal, on floes of ice, dozens of white isles, each with its own burden of souls marooned.

"I ain't seen him get out," said John.

"Seen who?"

"The captain."

"I doubt we'll see any more of him."

"Naw, he'll be fine."

"He went into the water, John. He's gone."

John looked troubled, but shrugged his shoulders and said again, "Naw, he'll be fine." He thought about it and added, "Jest fine. Come on, Thursty. Let's see we can't get over there and find some supplies. Might be a long ride home."

"Ride home? Ride *home*?"

"Where else you want to go? What about that lady back in Hally-fax?"

"The ship's sunk, John! We're dead. Both of us. All of us!"

"Naw, jest you stick close, Thursty. We be back in no time. Now if we was a little more north, we'd be at the mercy of them Indrawin' Seas and such. But I reckon we'll be jest fine. Look yonder. That ice is breakin' up and driftin' southerly. We ain't but to ride the ice, Thursty. All the way back to Hally-fax. Dead reckonin'!"

Thurston turned to walk away and leave John Obadiah to freeze and die alone, but when he turned he saw there was nowhere for him to go. The ice they stood on had broken free and they were marooned on a floe all their own. Thurston clenched his fists and wailed at the heavens.

"Dog *gone*, Thursty! Why you so *agg*ervated? Come on." John walked to the edge of the floe nearest the next, which was across some twenty feet of water.

"What are you doing?"

"Got to jump."

"Into the *water*?"

"Naw. Over to that ice yonder."

Thurston replied in a flat, humorless voice. "You're going to jump twenty feet. To that ice yonder. Of course you are."

"Why not?"

"There's no way you can jump that far."

"Whatchoo reckon will happen if I miss it?"

Thurston glared at John. "I '*reckon*' you'll end up wet."

"Then what?"

"Then you'll freeze or drown, one or the other in short order. Either way, I'll be rid of you." Thurston shook his head and then stopped and smiled viciously. "You know what, John? Go on. Please do. Jump, John Obadiah. Jump and let me be rid of you."

"It stands on good reason that I'll make that jump, Thursty. 'Cause that oracle ain't said nothin' about dyin' by cold nor water.

"I suppose you're going to walk on water, are you?"

"You got no faith. That's yore problem, Thursty. Tell you what. Come on, jump on my back. I best take you with me so I ain't got to come back for you."

"What?"

"You want to be left here all by your lonesome?"

Thurston laughed, but it was a terrible and angry sound.

"Come on." John grabbed Thurston and tried to pick him up.

"Don't touch me, you imbecile!"

"It's for yer own good!"

Thurston broke free of John's grip and ran across the floe. John chased him and pawed at him and Thurston cried out and yelled for help, though he couldn't have said from whence help might come.

63

Finally, John took hold of him by the neck of his coat the way a gentle bitch carries her pups.

"I got yeh."

Thurston sagged, winded, too tired to struggle free. "Leave me be."

"I cain't leave you here, Thursty. Wouldn't set right."

John leaned over and threw his shoulder into Thurston's middle. Too surprised by the assault to resist, Thurston bent double and folded over onto John's back. As he went down, he saw, as if time itself had slowed to provide him the view, a thumb-sized scar on John's forehead which passed out of sight as he fell, followed by a bald patch of hair on the back of John's head and another, twin, scar. John stood up with one arm clenched around Thurston's knee. Before Thurston could protest or muster the energy to resist, John grunted and heaved himself into a run straight for the edge of the floe.

Then they were in the air. John ascended into his leap and Thurston saw nothing but water beneath them. For Thurston, time was still passing drowsily by and he measured and observed each moment in both horror and fascination. He noted first that John's leap was no graceful flight like that of a doe, but something more akin to the inelegant hop of a fat toad. And the great leap was not only ungraceful, it was also far, far short. Almost as soon as they began their ascent, the arc of the leap failed, and as the two men plummeted toward the grey sea, Thurston heard the distinct and odious sound of Obadiah giggling. When he heard that stupid giggle, he gathered a brief satisfaction from the knowledge that Obadiah was about to be proven, at long last, to be a fool, and something in Thurston exulted in the fact that John would plunge into the cold sea whilst giggling in his preposterous confidence. Thurston resigned himself to the shock of sudden cold and the death sure to follow, and then, suddenly, the water below him was transfigured. It rose up like a bubble and a slick black form emerged from it. John Obadiah's descending feet came down firmly on whaleflesh. "Hoooo! Heeeeee!"

As John Obadiah landed on the whale, the blowhole opened and spewed out a geyser of seawater that struck Thurston in the face. The shock of the cold water snapped time back into its proper rhythm and Thurston was left staring wide-eyed and speechless at the impossibility of his own salvation. The whale beneath them surged forward and John leapt once more, this time from the whale to the opposite ice floe. He landed squarely, took a few short steps, and then set Thurston down on his feet as the whale dove and threw its tail high as if in salutation.

"Come on, Thursty. Let's get some food and such."

Thurston wiped his face and looked at John Obadiah, dumbfounded. "That's impossible."

"Yeah, but that ain't stopped it."

As John walked off toward the next ice floe, Thurston was overcome by a sense of lightness. The two men ran, leaping from floe to floe, and Thurston no longer gave any thought to how far the leap might be, he simply leapt when leaping was needed. And each time, he found he had crossed the distance with ease, though he was glad that none of the floes they leapt onto were more than a few feet away. He kept his eyes on John's back, and in a few minutes they'd managed to find a route across the broken floes to where the ship's salvaged supplies were being divided

out amongst the crew. Don Fuego nodded to John as they approached and apportioned them each a blanket, a bundle of sea rations, and a tent to share.

"Now what?" asked Thurston.

"Ship gone," said Don Fuego. "Captain gone. Who can say?"

"Captain *gone*?" asked John.

Don Fuego nodded his head. "With ship."

John's forehead wrinkled up, and for the first time, Thurston thought he spotted what might be a frown. "Naw, he'll turn up."

AFTER THE SINKING OF THE *MARIBEL LYNNE* AND

the loss of her unfailing captain, the crew broke into small groups and followed whatever course of action seemed best. The weather's fair turn was short lived. Temperatures plummeted and, within a week, the pack ice conglomerated and solidified once more and made for safer travel. Some of the men stayed put, camped on the ice and waiting for rescue. Others set out afoot, hoping to cross the ice fields and find landfall to the south. For Thurston's part, he followed after John Obadiah, sticking close beside him, and for John Obadiah's part, he aimed himself toward "Hally-fax" and swore to return Thurston safely to Belinda Lee.

After two weeks alone on the ice, travel became a monotony of walking, sleeping, and slowly starving. The prospect of starvation did not trouble John at all, and it troubled Thurston very little in the wake of John's leap. But as they pressed south toward civilization, spring slowly overtook winter and the ice began again to thaw.

In late April, Thurston and John found themselves marooned on a solitary floe of ice borne gently southward, yet melting steadily, day by day. Thurston often looked about him and saw only grey-black sea and felt certain their deaths were nigh, but in those times he reassured himself with the memory of that slick grey whale breaching the deep and spraying its magnanimous breath upon him.

After two weeks afloat on the dwindling floe, they were rescued. A small whaling ship named *Queenie Marie* came upon them in heavy seas. The swells heaved up and down like mountains around them, and though the ship was intent on rescue, it was unlikely they'd chance a second pass. The *Queenie Marie's* crew hung a net over the side and when they passed nearest the floe, John Obadiah leapt from the ice, grabbed the net, and pulled himself aboard. As Thurston prepared a leap of his own, a swell pushed the floe away and the distance to the ship widened to a perilous stretch. Thurston gave it no thought. He looked up and saw John at the rail and noted once more the round scar on his forehead. Thurston leapt. He wondered as he did if there were a whale of his own lurking in wait beneath the waves, but he thought little of it because his leap alone had been enough. His fingers caught in the net and he climbed aboard.

Thurston and John Obadiah grinned at each another and laughed as the captain of the *Queenie Marie* ordered coats brought, beds prepared, and food warmed.

"You're lucky we spotted you," said the captain, a rotund man with a bulbous nose.

John Obadiah chuckled and Thurston said, "We'll be luckier yet if we're bound for Halifax, sir. I've an appointment to keep with a patient young lady."

"Then your luck is double indeed. We'll berth in Halifax before the week is out."

"I tole you so, Thursty."

Before Thurston could answer, the ship's bell rang out.

"Iceberg," cried the helmsman.

Ahead of the ship a small mountain of ice drifted toward them. Rain washed down its surface, polishing it, sluicing it clean and clear as a lens, and at the heart of the berg: a shape. The crew lined the rail, leaning forward intently to watch the passing giant and inspect the strange form frozen within it. The closer the iceberg loomed, the more certain was Thurston of what he saw. Frozen into the heart of the ice was an enormous white shark. The beast had been seized in the attitude of attack, its body curled as if its tail had been stopped just as it was to whip around and propel the animal toward its prey. The beast was fearsome, its maw wide and finely toothed, but it was its prey that held all who saw it transfixed. In opposition to the shark's attack, there loomed the form of a man, his back arched, his mouth twisted into a snarl, and one arm thrown high. In his raised fist, the frozen man clutched a walrus-tooth knife, and over his shoulders flowed a thick white, fur coat. He had been arrested in the throes of mortal strife, captured like a sculpture enfleshed, a living icon of man and beast embattled. How the battle may have ended, none who saw it could say, for the man seemed the equal of the beast, and the beast the equal of the man—though neither the equal of the polar ice

Thurston's grin faded.

He turned to John Obadiah, who lowered his eyebrows, shook his head thoughtfully, and said, "Huh. I reckon that oracle was wrong after all."

RABBIT ROOM
— PRESS —

NASHVILLE, TENNESSEE